**What was Indiana Jones doing
in Turkey in June 1914?**

Indiana Jones is that world-famous, whip-cracking hero you know from the movies....

But was he *always* cool and fearless in the face of danger? Did he *always* get mixed up in hair-raising, heart-stopping adventures?

**Yes!**

Read all about Indy as a kid in Turkey on the eve of war....See him land in deep trouble with a bloodthirsty underground cult....And get ready for some nonstop, edge-of-your-seat excitement!

## Young Indiana Jones books

# YOUNG INDIANA JONES and the SECRET CITY

### By Les Martin

Random House New York

Young Indy novels are conceived and produced by Random House, Inc.,
in conjunction with Lucasfilm Ltd.

Library of Congress Cataloging-in-Publication Data
Martin, Les, 1934–
    Young Indiana Jones and the secret city / by Les Martin.
        p.   cm.
    Summary: Visiting Turkey in 1914, young Indiana Jones and his pal
Herman stumble onto an evil cult that lives in a secret underground city.
    ISBN 0-679-80580-X (pbk.) ISBN 0-679-90580-4 (lib. bdg.)
    [1. Adventure and adventurers—Fiction.] I. Title.
PZ7.M36353Ym   1990
[Fic]—dc20  89-43391 CIP AC

Manufactured in the United States of America    3 4 5 6 7 8 9 10

# YOUNG INDIANA JONES™

### and the

## SECRET CITY

# Chapter 1

"Constantinople," young Indiana Jones said. His eyes opened wide. The capital of Turkey was showing through the morning mist.

"It sure isn't Salt Lake City," said his friend Herman. He shook his head in wonder. Domes and towers were outlined against the brightening sky.

The two fourteen-year-old boys stood at the railing of a Greek tramp steamboat. It had brought them, along with Indy's dad, Professor Henry Jones, there from New York.

Its paint was peeling and its hull was rusty. Even its crew was ragged. Indy's dad did not believe in paying for a costly trip. Not when his money could be spent on rare books instead.

Professor Jones was in his cabin reading one of those books now. He had been there most of the trip. Across the Atlantic. Through the Strait of Gibraltar. Across the Mediterranean and the Aegean, with stops at Marseilles, Naples, and Athens. Up the narrow strip of water of the Dardanelles and through the choppy Sea of Marmara. Then to the crowded harbor of one of the most fabulous cities on earth.

"I can't believe I'm here," Herman said, still shaking his head. "I can't believe you talked me into this."

Indy grinned at his friend. It hadn't taken much talking to persuade Herman to come along with him. Indy was Herman's hero. He was everything that Herman wanted to be, lean and quick and daring. Herman followed him around like a puppy. A plump and panting puppy that tripped over its own feet trying to keep up with Indy.

Indy's dad had asked him to find a friend to take on this trip. Indy had thought of Herman right away. Professor Jones wanted Indy to have someone to do things with. He wanted Indy out of his hair while he was doing his research in Turkey on the Crusades. It was bad enough that he had to bring Indy with him. That was because the aunt who was supposed to take care of Indy during summer vacation fell sick.

For Indy, Herman was the perfect choice. Herman would go along with whatever Indy wanted to do. The worst Herman might do was urge caution. And Indy was good at turning a deaf ear to that.

Now Indy filled Herman's ears with what he had learned about Constantinople.

"It's the only city that's half in Europe and half in Asia," Indy said. "It was first built by the ancient Greeks. They called it Byzantium. Then it became the capital of the East Roman Empire. That's when it got the name of Constantinople. It kept that name when the Ottoman Turks made it capital of their empire."

Indy's eyes brightened. "But some Turks

now want to give it a new name. A modern name. A really Turkish name. Istanbul. I hope they do. Turkey has to leave the past behind and get up-to-date."

"Hey, for a guy who complains about your dad reading so much, you've sure read up on this place," Herman said.

"Look, I like books," Indy said. "In fact, I love books. But not the way my dad does. I use them to find out about the world around me. Not hide away from it."

At that moment, a voice from behind them called, "Junior!"

Indy turned and said, "I've told you, Dad, I don't want to be called that."

"But it's your name. Henry Jones, *Junior*," said Professor Henry Jones.

"Indiana is the name I go by," Indy insisted.

"Indiana was the name of our *dog*," said his dad.

"That dog gave his life to save me from a rattler," Indy said. "I owe it to him to keep his name alive. Besides, Indiana has a nice ring to it. A lot better than Junior."

"I have no time to argue now," Professor Jones said. "We dock soon. You and Herman better get packed."

"We already are," Indy said.

"Indy woke me at dawn," said Herman. He yawned. "I think I'll catch some shut-eye when we get to the hotel."

"No way," Indy said. "There's too much to see in this city. Too much to do."

"I agree," his dad said. "It has a splendid library. I can hardly wait to get a look at it."

Four hours later, their bags were at the Pera Palace Hotel. It was a splendid structure that welcomed travelers from the West. But Herman got only a longing look at the big feather bed in his room. He barely had a chance to wash up before Indy dragged him outside.

"At last," said Indy. "We're on our own. Dad will be in the state library until they throw him out for the night."

"Uh, Indy," said Herman, hanging back.

"What?" Indy asked impatiently.

"Remember what your dad made you promise him, just before he left us?" Herman said.

Indy scratched his head. "Can't seem to. He's always making me promise *some*thing."

"I'll remind you," Herman said. "He made you promise to watch your step and stay out of danger."

"Oh, *that,*" Indy said with a grin. "Sure I plan to watch my step. That's the best way to handle danger."

And with Herman close behind him, he plunged into the crowd. The flow of people streamed through streets that twisted like question marks in the vast city.

# Chapter 2

"Hey, let's not get lost," Herman said. His legs were shorter than Indy's. He had to half trot to keep up with Indy's long steps.

"We won't," said Indy. "I've been studying a map."

Their first stop was the most famous building in Constantinople. The Hagia Sophia. They gazed up at its huge dome. Many birds fluttered and swooped in the bright blue sky around it.

"Great, huh," said Indy. His voice was filled with awe. "It once was one of the greatest Christian churches in the world. When the Turks conquered the city in the 1400s, they were smart enough to leave the church alone. And to use it for their religion. It's now an Islamic church. A mosque."

Indy pointed to another big mosque across a large square. "That's the Blue Mosque. The Turks built that to try to outdo the Hagia Sophia."

"That's a lot of mosque," said Herman.

"Constantinople has a lot of Islamic believers," said Indy. "And there are a lot of other beautiful mosques all over town. We can see them all. Plus the Grand Bazaar, where everything in the world is for sale. And the outside of Topkapi Palace. That's where the Turkish sultan lives, though the new government took away his power."

"Do we have to do all this *today*?" Herman said. "Oh, my aching feet."

Just then a man's wailing voice cut through the air. People poured into the Hagia Sophia.

"What's that?" asked Herman.

"The call to prayer," said Indy. "Islamic believers go to prayer five times a day."

"I hope they don't mind us watching them," Herman said uneasily. "We're strangers."

"They won't, as long as we show respect for their religion," Indy said. "They're used to strangers here. Foreigners have been coming to trade or just see the city for thousands of years."

"Then it'll still be here tomorrow, right?" said Herman. "I mean, if we go to bed early, we can get an early start."

Indy took pity on his friend. "Okay, we'll head back to the hotel. We can check out the ships in the harbor on our way. They come from every country in the world."

Indy brought Herman to a halt in the middle of a bridge. They had to cross it to get back to their hotel. The bridge went over the Golden Horn, an arm of water that divided the city. From the bridge they could see flags of many nations fluttering on many kinds of ships.

"Why all the warships?" Herman wondered. "There's an English one. And a French. A German. And what's that one there?"

"A Russian," Indy said. "All the European powers have a stake in Turkey. They want it on their side in case of war among them."

"Never happen," said Herman. "My dad says there's no chance of a big war ever again. I mean, this is 1914. The world's too civilized to blow itself apart."

"That so?" said Indy. He looked at the gun barrels jutting out of all the warships. He shook his head. Then he spotted something more interesting.

A small white cutter was being lowered into the water. It came from a large gray battleship flying the Russian flag. Indy watched as the sailors in the cutter cast off its lines. Then they started rowing. What was interesting was that the cutter did not head for the shore. Instead, it made a beeline to another cutter waiting offshore.

"Wonder what's going on," mused Indy.

"None of our business," Herman said quickly. "Time to get back to our hotel."

"No harm in watching a little more," said Indy.

"Famous last words," said Herman with

16

a sigh. But he didn't waste breath arguing. When Indy sensed a mystery, nothing would stop him from pursuing it.

"Take a look at that guy in the second cutter," said Indy.

It was hard not to look at the man Indy was talking about. He was tall, about seven feet, towering over the men rowing his boat. He was built like a bear and weighed at least three hundred pounds. He had a bushy black beard. And he wore a black suit that must have needed a tentmaker to tailor it.

The bearded man reached out a hand. He took a leather bag from a naval officer commanding the first cutter. As soon as the delivery was made, the cutters separated. The first cutter headed back to the warship. The second headed for the shore.

"Let's find out more," said Indy. "This city is supposed to be a hotbed of foreign intrigue. Maybe we can see some firsthand."

Herman had no chance to protest. Indy led the way across the bridge to where the second cutter was heading.

Indy and Herman reached the spot before

the cutter did. They pretended to inspect the wares of a street jewelry vendor as the boat docked. The bearded man climbed out with the leather bag in his hand.

It was easy to tail the huge man as he shoved his way through the crowded streets. After a while, Herman observed, "You know, this route looks familiar."

"It is," said Indy. "That's our hotel dead ahead."

"And the big guy's going into it," said Herman.

"Maybe we can find out what room he's in at the reception desk," said Indy.

"And maybe we can leave well enough alone," said Herman.

"Come on, where's your curiosity?" said Indy.

"Ever heard of curiosity and the cat?" snapped Herman.

"I'm a dog person myself," said Indy.

"Yeah, a bloodhound," said Herman.

But Indy did not make it to the reception desk. His father, who had been waiting in the lobby, cut him off.

"Thank goodness you finally got back," Professor Jones said. "I hope you haven't unpacked yet."

"No," said Indy. "Why?"

"We're moving out of here right away," said his dad.

"You don't like the hotel?" asked Herman with a sigh. The feather bed had looked so beautiful!

"Hotel?" said Professor Jones. "What could that have to do with it? I'm talking about something important. Books. The library here doesn't have the ones I need. They're in Konya. There's an overnight train leaving for there in an hour."

"Did you get a sleeping car?" asked Herman hopefully.

"There isn't one," Professor Jones said. "Doesn't really matter, though. The trip isn't bad. Just twelve hours. I can finish some background reading I still have to do."

"Get ready for a nice cattle car ride, Herman," Indy advised. "Dad buys just one kind of tickets anywhere. The cheapest kind."

"Actually, I had to buy first-class tickets,"

his dad said. "Highway robbery. But that was all that was left. And we were lucky to get even them. Somebody canceled reservations at the last minute. Now let's get moving. If we miss this train, we wait two days for another."

They arrived at the railway station with ten minutes to spare. Smoke was already belching out of their locomotive. A man naked to the waist was shoveling coal into the engine furnace.

A porter led them to their compartment. Two faded red plush seats faced two others.

"At least we have a spare seat," said Herman, after they stowed their luggage in the overhead rack. "There's space for *one* of us to stretch out and take a nap. Hint, hint."

"Pleasant dreams," said Indy. Beside him, his dad opened a book. Indy opened a book of his own.

"I'll do my best," said Herman, stretching out and closing his eyes.

A minute later, he was yanked out of dreamland. The compartment door slid noisily open.

Filling the doorway was a huge figure of a man. A familiar figure. Seven feet tall, three hundred pounds, with a bushy black beard, and a leather bag in his hand.

The man looked at the three of them with a searching gaze, and Herman felt a chill run through him.

# Chapter 3

"*Deutsch? Français?* English?" the bearded man asked.

Professor Jones reluctantly looked up from his book. "We're Americans," he said.

"I am Russian," the man said. "Fyodor Rostov, dealer in superior carpets, at your service."

"I'm Henry Jones," said the professor. "This is my son, Henry, Junior. And his friend, Herman Mueller."

"Indiana," said Indy.

"Ah, you come from the state of Indiana," said Rostov.

"No, that's my name—the one I go by," said Indy.

"I understand. My friends, they call me Fedya," said Rostov. "You are going to Konya? Very unusual for Americans."

"I'm doing a study on the Crusades," Professor Jones explained. "Right now, I'm investigating the Seljuk Turks. They opposed the Crusaders moving along the Turkish coast toward Palestine. Their capital was Konya."

Meanwhile, Indy shot Herman a warning look. *Be careful,* it said. *Don't let on what we know about this guy.*

"Ah, you like history," Rostov said to the professor. By now he had dragged in a huge case from the passageway outside. He tossed it up on the luggage rack as if it were light as a feather.

Then Rostov settled his huge body in the seat beside Herman. He kept his leather bag on his lap. "Konya is very good for that. In Konya the old ways are very much alive."

Professor Jones shrugged. "I don't care about that. Just so long as they've kept their old manuscripts in good shape."

Indy, though, was interested. Besides, he wanted to find out all he could about this fellow Rostov. "I've been reading about the whirling dervishes," he said. "Are they still around in Konya?"

"The whirling dervishes?" asked Herman.

"They're an Islamic sect," said Indy. "They do a whirling dance to increase their religious feeling."

"Actually, my going to Konya has a lot to do with them," said Professor Jones. "Their founder was a great poet and preacher named Mevlana. He lived in Konya. I want to learn how he and his followers felt about the crusaders."

Professor Jones turned to Indy. "You can come to the library with me and find out all you want about the dervishes."

"The library?" said Indy. He wrinkled his nose in distaste. "Come all this way to go to a library?"

"You should listen to your father," Rostov advised, as the train whistle blew. There was a sharp jerk, and the train started moving. "Konya is different from Constantinople. Its people are not so used to foreigners. In fact, they are quite suspicious of strangers. They can be unfriendly. *Very* unfriendly."

"Hey, maybe the library isn't a bad idea," said Herman. "I mean, it's quiet in a library. And cool. And *safe*. You can probably find a picture of those dervishes there."

"I already have a picture," said Indy. He showed Herman the book he was reading. In it was a drawing of a man in a floor-length white robe. It was tied tight at the waist with a sash. Below the waist the robe swirled out like a flaring skirt as the man whirled in his dance. On his head was a tall cone hat. It made him look like a wizard or a magician.

"But a picture isn't the real thing," Indy pointed out. "I want to see a dervish in action."

Rostov chuckled. "You are a boy with a sense of adventure. And an active imagination. I must say, I was amused when I saw you and your friend today. When you followed me this afternoon."

"You *saw* us?" Indy said, suddenly feeling a little silly.

"Of course I did," Rostov said. "A merchant like me has to have a sharp eye. I often carry large sums of money and must be on my guard. I spotted you two at once. In your Western clothes, you stuck out like sore thumbs."

Rostov saw the dismay on Indy's face. He chuckled again. "I can imagine what you thought when you saw the Russian officer handing me this bag. I bet you were sure you had stumbled onto some kind of spy ring. That's what comes of reading too many dime novels. They make things seem so much more romantic and exciting than they really are."

Rostov smiled. "Actually, the man was just delivering payment. For carpets used to decorate the admiral's quarters. But if you had known that, you wouldn't have been able to play your little game. More fun than playing cowboys and Indians, eh?"

"I hope they didn't bother you," Professor Jones said.

"Not at all," Rostov said. "Boys will be boys."

"And I hope this will be a lesson to you,

Junior," the professor said to Indy. "You're too old for such childish nonsense. And I certainly don't want you involved in any more high jinks when we get to Konya."

"Right. I've learned my lesson," said Indy, and buried himself in his book.

"I hope so," his dad repeated as he opened his book again. "I don't have time to bail you out of any trouble. Not to mention possibly losing my library pass. It was devilishly hard to get."

"I hope so, too," said Rostov. "Believe me, it could be very dangerous for boys like you to wander through strange parts of the city."

Herman, too, hoped Indy had learned his lesson. Herman hoped to have a nice smooth trip from here on in, full of peace and quiet.

That hope stayed alive when they arrived the next morning in Konya. They checked into their hotel right away. Indy and Herman shared a twin-bedded room. Indy didn't object at all when Herman declared he was lying down on his bed and taking a little nap.

Bright sunlight coming through the window woke Herman up.

He looked around the room, and his heart sank.

So much for his hope that Indy had been cured of hunting adventure.

Indy was gone.

# Chapter 4

Herman sat up in bed. He should go find Indy. Maybe Indy was in a jam and needed help.

On the other hand, maybe he should just bury his head under the covers again. Herman thought about the foreign city, filled with unfriendly Turks, outside the hotel room door. Going back to bed seemed like a good idea.

"Time to get up!" Indy announced as he came into the room. "It's already afternoon. Don't want to waste the day."

"Why not?" Herman demanded. "Besides, who says sleep is a waste? It's necessary. I'm a growing boy."

"I hope you're big enough to fit into these," Indy said.

He tossed a white cotton shirt and trousers onto Herman's bed.

"What are these?" Herman asked. "Where did you get them?"

"Used clothes," said Indy. "I got them at a stall in the local market."

By now Herman's eyes were focused. He could see that Indy was wearing similar clothes. They were clean but very worn.

"No sense standing out like sore thumbs when we explore the city," Indy explained. "You see, I did listen to Rostov. They're suspicious of strangers in Konya—so we'll make sure not to look strange."

"And what do we do for shoes?" Herman asked. "I think our Buster Browns will really stand out in this town."

"We won't wear any," said Indy. He pointed to his bare feet and wiggled his toes. "I saw a lot of street kids going barefooted.

And the poorer we look, the less anyone will notice us."

"But we don't look like Turks," Herman protested.

"And what do you think Turks look like?" said Indy impatiently. "Take a look around you when we're on the street. Turks come in all sizes, shapes, and colors. All kinds of people have made Turkey their home."

Herman gave up. His chances of winning this argument with Indy were zero to none. Groaning, he heaved himself up out of bed and put on the loose cotton clothes.

Barefoot, the two boys snuck down the richly carpeted hallway. Down the stairs. And out the hotel door before the desk clerk could give them more than a shake of his fist.

"See, he thought we were Turkish street kids," Indy said with a smile.

Then his face lit up even more.

"Herman, you see what I see?" he said.

Herman followed Indy's gaze. Walking down the street ahead of them was a man. He wore a tall cone hat and a long white robe.

"A dervish," said Indy. "Quick! After him. Maybe we can get to see him in action."

"I don't know," said Herman. "He might not be crazy about us spying on him."

"Don't *worry*," Indy said. "We'll tail him at a safe distance. We won't take any risks."

Keeping the dervish in sight, they moved through the bustling streets of the clean, well-ordered city. Around them peddlers hawked their wares. Farmers showed their fruits, vegetables, and squawking chickens. Boys ran to and fro with trays of tea in tiny glasses. All of them were busily going about their business as they had for centuries.

Herman thought how different it was from America. There, so many things were new and change was always in the air. He felt very, very far from home.

Indy, though, seemed right at home. He didn't stop as he threaded his way through the traffic. The streets were filled with horses and camels and men bearing huge loads of goods on their backs. Ahead of him he saw the dervish enter a small white building.

Indy moved faster, ignoring Herman's

panting protests. Reaching the building, Indy tried the doorknob.

"Don't *worry*," Indy said. "Just checking to see if the door is open." Then he said, "It *is*. Let's take a peek inside. If we're spotted, we can do a lost-tourist routine."

"In these clothes?" asked Herman.

"Don't *worry*," said Indy. "All we have to do is open our mouths, and they'll believe us."

Very slowly he opened the door a crack.

"That's funny," he said. "There just seems to be one big room, and it's empty."

He opened the door and stepped inside. Herman had nowhere to go but after him.

The room was white, empty, and bare of furniture. The only human touch was a small brightly colored, flat-woven rug on the floor.

"It's a prayer rug," said Indy. He bent to examine it more closely. He studied the woven design in green against a red background. It looked like a tree bare of leaves. "See this pattern. It's called a tree of life."

Then Indy knitted his brows. He pulled a compass from his pocket. "The tree should be pointed east, toward the holy city of Mecca. But this one isn't." He bent over and tugged at the rug. It was fastened down. As if it was being used to cover something. He felt along its edge. It *was* covering something.

"A trap door," Indy said. Slowly he lifted it. It came up easily, with the rug on top. He saw stairs leading downward.

*"Indy,"* Herman warned in a whisper.

"I told you, don't *worry*," Indy said. "Look, there are candles and matches. They can light our way."

"Great," said Herman. "I wouldn't like to think this was dangerous or anything."

Indy lit a candle. Then the boys went down the stairs, lowering the trap door above them. At the foot of the stairs was a passageway. At its end was a dimly lit doorway. Loud chanting in a foreign tongue came from it. Indy headed for the light, with Herman tiptoeing behind.

Indy and Herman peeked through the entrance. Their eyes opened wide.

In the center of a large room, the dervish

whirled faster and faster. In front of him an audience of perhaps twenty men chanted faster and faster. Behind him was a towering black stone statue. A statue of a monstrous man with an upraised hand. That hand held a knife—a knife with a bright red blade.

Indy backed away from the doorway. Herman did the same.

"Time to clear out," Herman whispered. "You've seen your whirling dervish."

Indy shook his head. "That was no whirling dervish. You see that statue? That idol? Islamic believers *hate* idols."

"Then who was that dancing guy—and those chanting people?" wondered Herman.

"I don't know," said Indy. "But I sure mean to find—"

At that moment, a huge hand clamped on his shoulder. Another clamped on Herman's.

# Chapter 5

Indy tried to wriggle free, but the hand on his shoulder held him like a vise. He turned his head to see a man's broad chest. He looked upward to see the face.

"Rostov!" he exclaimed. "What are you—"

"You will answer questions, not ask them," Rostov snarled.

With that, he pushed Indy and Herman into the room.

The dance of the false dervish stopped in mid-whirl. The chanting stopped, too. The false dervish spoke a few words in what must have been Turkish. Immediately the audience stood up and filed out of the room.

Rostov spoke to the false dervish in the same language. Then Rostov pushed the boys up against a wall and let go of them. But he stood in front of them, blocking all escape.

"You two, who are you spying for?" he demanded.

"We weren't spying," Indy said. "We were just—curious. You know how tourists are. Out to see the sights. Of course, if we offended you, we're sorry. Really sorry. Really, *really* sorry. Believe me."

"I believe you—about being sorry," said Rostov. "You're sorry you were caught. But not as sorry as you're going to be."

"But, like I told you—" began Indy.

"Let *me* tell *you* something," Rostov said. "I saw you come out of the hotel wearing disguises. I saw you following this man here. I saw you sneaking into this house."

"And we never saw you," said Indy. He was playing for time. And looking for information. "Hey, you're the one who's good at spying."

Rostov drew himself up to his full immense height. "Far better than you. His Imperial Majesty does not employ children to do a man's work."

"His Imperial Majesty?" said Indy.

"Nicholas the Second," said Rostov.

"The Czar of Russia himself," said Indy, acting impressed. "Hey, I bet you're not really a rug merchant named Rostov. You have to be somebody important. Somebody high up."

"Count Igor Ivanovich Stravsky," said the Russian. Then he gave a rumbling chuckle. "I dare say you think you are very clever— getting this information from me. As if I would be fooled by such a childish trick."

"Sorry," said Indy. "I'll try to do better next time."

Count Igor did not find this amusing. "There is only one reason that I have spoken so freely," he said grimly. "Can you guess what that reason is?"

Indy gulped. "I guess so. Then again, sometimes I have a kind of wild imagination."

"I will save you the guesswork," Count Igor said. "I can tell you anything I want, because I don't have to worry about your telling anybody else."

"That's right. We won't tell anybody else. Scout's honor," said Herman eagerly.

"Uhh, Herman, I don't think that's exactly what the count here means," said Indy.

"I won't even waste time asking you about your spying," said Count Igor. "You Americans cannot be taken seriously. A childish people, and so far away from the rest of the world."

"Real far away. Too far away to be interested in doing any spying here," Indy suggested.

"And too far away to find out what happened to two little American boys," Count Igor said. He pulled a leather thong from his pocket. "You know what this is?"

Indy looked at it. "Well, it's pretty thick to be a shoelace."

"I picked this up on a mission to Spain," Count Igor said fondly. "It's called a garrote. A marvelous tool. I've used it many times. It's light, fits in the pocket, leaves no mess. I simply hook it around a neck, give a sharp pull on both ends, and—it never fails to do the job."

"Hey, neat. What won't they think up next," said Indy. He looked for some way to make a break for it. All he could see was Count Igor's huge body. Getting around him was impossible. Trying to slug him would be like punching a stone wall. He couldn't think of anything to do, anything to say.

Herman could, though.

"You can't do this!" Herman protested. "We're innocent!"

It was better than nothing, Indy thought. Not much better, though.

Still, Indy joined in. "That's right. You can't do this. We're innocent!"

Count Igor shrugged. "You say I can't. I say I can. There is only one way to see who is right."

He moved toward Indy, his garrote at the ready.

Nothing stood between Indy and death.

Nothing but one word.

"Stop!" the false dervish ordered. He knew English. The sweetest word in the language.

Count Igor lowered the garrote.

"You two boys, you swear you are innocent?" the false dervish demanded.

"Yes sir," said Indy. "Absolutely. Totally. Completely. Scout's honor."

Herman was more convincing. There was no doubting the sincerity in his cracking voice. "Honest, we haven't done *any*thing."

"I believe you," the man said. "You are innocent, both of you. Two young innocents."

He smiled. But that smile did not make Indy feel better. Instead it made him shudder. The man's teeth were filed in sharp points. His jet-black beard was sharply pointed, too. The mirror image of a devil's. His eyes were just as black. They seemed to jab into Indy like daggers.

"Thank you, sir, thank you," said Herman. He was almost whimpering, he was so grateful.

Indy expected Count Igor would be angry

to have his fun spoiled. But the count smiled a nasty smile of his own.

"I wouldn't give thanks too soon," Count Igor said. And his laugh boomed like thunder before a storm.

# Chapter 6

"Enough," the false dervish said, cutting off the count's laughter. "I have what I need. Now let us get out of here. We do not have much time. Only a few days."

"Yes, Your Highness," Count Igor replied.

" 'Your Highness'?" Indy asked the false dervish. "You some kind of king?"

The false dervish drew himself up proudly. "*Some* kind of king?" he said. "I am *the* king. The King of Kings. King Zed."

"The king of kings, huh?" said Indy. He tuned to the count. "And where does that put your boss, the czar?"

The count smiled. "Clever boy, playing for time. And trying to drive a wedge between me and the king," he said. "Let me assure you, my master the czar and the king here are the best of friends. That is why I am here—to give the king any help he may need."

"You can give me some of that help now," the man who called himself King Zed declared. "Tie the boys up. And get the caravan ready. We will leave town as soon as it gets dark."

"Your wish is my command," said the count.

He bowed deeply to the king. Then he took a coil of thin wire from his pocket. He used it to tie up Indy hand and foot. He did the same to Herman.

"I won't bother gagging you," the count said. "You can shout as loud as you want. But no one will hear you down here. See you soon, boys. Then we'll all take a little trip together."

He and the king left the room. As soon as they were gone, Herman said, "Good thing they don't know you, Indy. I bet you've already figured out a way to get us untied and out of here. Right, Indy?" There was a silence. Herman repeated, "Indy?"

"Uhh, well, not exactly," Indy said. "This wire is kind of tough. Strong as steel. And it'll cut into us if we try to move."

"But you'll come up with something, right?" Herman said. He did his best to put a lot of hope in his voice. He wasn't successful.

"Sure. At some point," Indy said. "But we'll have to wait for our chance. Anyway, I want to find out what's happening between this count and this king. I'm really dying to know."

"And we might die *to* know. Ever hear the saying, what you don't know can't hurt you?" said Herman. He looked at Indy. Then he sighed. "No, guess you haven't."

He didn't have a chance to say more. The count returned to the room. With him were four powerfully built men. They were carrying two large Oriental carpets.

"Did you boys have a nice chat?" said the

count. "I hope you agreed not to try to escape. You wouldn't succeed. And you would be punished most severely. So I suggest you relax and enjoy your trip. It will be a real treat for boys like you. Boys so curious about the world. You will get to see things that only a chosen few have ever seen before. And you will have the thrill of helping to make history, not just learning about it."

"Thanks a lot," said Indy with a pained smile. He felt as though he was being forced to eat his own words.

"Don't mention it," said the count. He nodded to his men, and they unrolled the carpets. They laid one boy in each of them. Then they rolled the carpets around the boys like cocoons.

From inside the carpet Indy heard the count say, "Snug as a bug in a rug, boys. But don't worry. We won't crush you. Or even let you smother. We want to keep you alive—for the time being."

Indy felt himself being picked up. He did not know how far he was carried. It felt like a voyage on a storm-tossed boat. Then it ended with a jarring thud. He was still all in one piece, but barely. Then there was another motion, up and down, up and down. He wondered if you could get seasick on dry land.

Finally he felt his carpet being lifted up and set down again. He was rolled over and over as the carpet was unrolled. At last it was off him. He looked up to see a camel's face looking down at him curiously.

Next to the camel stood the count and the king. Both of them wore the flowing robes and hoods of Arab desert tribesmen. The men around them were dressed the same way and held rifles in their hands. Indy turned his head. Next to him lay Herman. Herman was yawning. Somehow he had managed to grab a nap.

"Shoot," said Herman. "I was hoping this was all a bad dream."

"You will not have a chance to dream for some time," said the count. "We are riding all night."

The count barked an order to one of his men. The man untied the boys while his comrades kept their rifles at the ready. Then the count tossed the boys Arab robes like the ones everyone else wore.

"Put these on," the count said. "We will make better time with you riding in the saddle."

"Pretty good disguises," Indy commented. "These hoods keep anybody we meet from seeing your faces or ours. And you can pass for Arab rug merchants heading home. We are heading east, aren't we?"

"Such a clever boy," said the count. "You never get tired of trying to make me tell you things. But don't worry. You will find out soon enough where we are going."

"Enough talking. Saddle up," the king commanded. "We do not have time to waste. We have to reach my city in time."

"In time for what?" asked Indy. "Some kind of party?"

At this the king laughed. "Yes, some kind of party," he said.

"And we're invited?" said Indy.

"*Invited?*" said the King. "Why, you're more than invited. You boys will be the guests of honor."

# Chapter 7

The light of dawn was spreading over the land. Riding together on a fast-stepping camel, Herman and Indy blinked at what they saw.

"This time I *know* I'm dreaming," Herman said.

"Some dream," said Indy, shaking his head in wonder.

The caravan had traveled through the night. Then through the day. Then through the next night. They had rested only a few hours in the midday heat. Their path had cut through a vast plain of wheat rippling like a golden sea in the breeze. This was Turkey's version of Kansas or Nebraska, where hardworking farmers fed a nation. But now, after the second night of travel, the boys saw a far different landscape.

"What a lot of rocks," said Herman.

"And *what* rocks," said Indy.

There were gigantic rocks as far as the eye could see. Rocks that looked like towering chimneys. Rocks that looked like monster mushrooms. Rocks that looked like huge pointed hats. Rocks that looked as if they had been shaped from sand by giant children. Children using toy shovels and buckets and wild imaginations. It was a scene right out of a fairy tale.

"Cappadocia," said Indy.

"Cappa-what?" said Herman.

"Cappadocia," said Indy. "It's a region in Turkey. I've read about it. See those big mountains way off on the horizon?"

Herman squinted into the rising sun. He nodded.

"They used to be volcanoes," Indy said. "A

few million years ago, they erupted. They spread hot lava over this whole region. That lava cooled into soft volcanic rock. Then rain and wind went to work."

"It's weird, like nature went crazy," Herman said. "I've never seen anything like it."

"Know what I see when I look at those rocks?" said Indy.

"I don't know," said Herman. "Castles? Towers? Bridges? It could be anything."

"What I see is hiding places," Indy said.

"You mean . . ." Herman asked.

Indy nodded.

". . . we make a run for it?" Herman said. The guard on the camel behind them spoke no English. But Herman lowered his voice anyway. "Maybe that's not such a hot idea. I mean, why make waves? That King Zed guy said he wanted us to be guests of honor at some kind of party. That doesn't sound so bad."

"Do you remember his smile when he said it?" said Indy. "And the gleam in his eyes?"

"Yeah, guess it doesn't look so good," said

Herman with a sigh. "But how do we get away? That fellow behind us has a mean-looking face. And an even meaner-looking rifle."

"He's also half asleep," said Indy. "This has been a tough trip."

"Funny. I should be as sleepy as him—but I'm not," said Herman, looking puzzled. "In fact, I've never felt so wide awake in my life. I mean, that's not *like* me."

"Maybe you've finally woken up to the danger we're in," said Indy. "Danger does that. Keeps you on your toes. That's what I like about it."

"Not me. What I usually like is a nice safe spot for a good long nap," said Herman. "But until I find one, I'm with you, Indy. When do we make our break?"

"Let's see," said Indy. He paused, thinking it over. Then he said, "What about— *now*!"

Reaching into his Arab robe, he pulled out a whip he had hidden there.

"Where did you get—" Herman began. He didn't have time to finish his question. Indy gave the camel a whack, the way he had seen the native riders do. It worked. The camel broke into a gallop as Indy gave its reins a sharp yank to the right.

They raced around a nearby rock. A bullet splintered the rock above their heads as they made the turn. Then they were behind the rock, protected for a moment.

"From here on, we play hide-and-seek," Indy said. His eyes swept the area. He spotted a narrow gap between two gigantic rocks. He used his whip again. The camel gave a snort of protest but instantly started racing for the gap across a stretch of open ground. They were followed by shouts and gunfire and men on camels in hot pursuit.

"This baby can really move," gasped Indy as they reached the gap. "Trouble is, it's kind of clumsy for dodging and dashing. We'd be better off on foot."

Indy reined the camel to a halt, and the boys jumped off. They went through the gap and found themselves in a canyon winding between two walls of rock.

"Just one way to go," said Indy. He started

running. Not as fast as he could, though. He had to make sure Herman could keep up as they fled their pursuers.

The boys rounded a bend in the canyon.

Then they slowed down. They had come upon a field planted with grapes.

"A little vineyard," said Indy with interest. "Every tiny bit of soil around here must be used to grow crops."

But Herman wasn't interested in local farming methods. He was interested in one thing only.

"That means there must be people around here," he said. "People who can help us out of this jam." He looked around him. "But where are they? I haven't seen a house anywhere."

"Yes you have—except you didn't know it," said Indy. He pointed to the rock cliff on the left. "See what I see?"

Herman's mouth dropped open.

"It's a door," he said.

"This rock is soft—easy to hollow out for homes," Indy said. "That's where the folk around here must live. Inside the rocks."

The boys ran to it. The door was made of wood and looked very old.

"No time to knock," said Indy. He heard the voices of their pursuers coming closer. He pushed at the door to see if it was unlocked.

It was. Indy had to bend his head a little to go through the doorway. The local people had to be quite short. Unless this really was some kind of fairyland filled with elves.

He and Herman entered a spotlessly clean room. It had simple furniture and beautiful rugs on the floor. And inside the room were two very real people.

A very old woman dressed in black. And a very young baby dressed in nothing. Both of them stared at Indy and Herman with very big eyes.

First Indy turned to close the door. Then he turned back to the old woman and the baby. At that moment, he realized he still had the whip clutched in one hand.

Hurriedly he stuck it back inside his robe. He held his hands palms up to show he meant these people no harm.

He didn't get a chance to tell them anything else.

There was a loud pounding on the door. And angry voices. Indy recognized one of them. The count's.

"I know you're in there! Give up! You're trapped!"

# Chapter 8

Indy looked desperately around the room for a way out. Nothing. Then his eyes met the old woman's. And a surprising thing happened. Seeing as how he and Herman were strangers. Strangers who had barged in bringing trouble. She smiled.

It was a toothless smile in a wrinkled face. But it was the most beautiful smile Indy had ever seen.

The woman motioned for Indy and Herman to follow her. Carrying the baby in one arm, she pushed aside a curtain. And led them into the kitchen. It had a fireplace and shelves filled with dishes. Huge copper and brass pots and pans hung on the walls.

The woman went to the back wall. She pushed aside a brightly colored rug hanging on it. Behind the rug was a door even smaller than the one in front. She opened it. Indy saw daylight.

"Thanks," Indy said. Then he remembered one of the few phrases in Turkish he had picked up. The phrase to learn in any language. Thank you. *"Tesekkurederim."*

*"Birsey degil,"* answered the old woman. That had to mean, "You're welcome." She smiled again. She touched her forehead and then her heart and bowed.

Indy and Herman did the same. Then they were out the door and running.

Going through the back door had gotten them out of the canyon. But they were still in a trackless world of huge rocks. They had plenty of cover. But no idea where they were heading. They knew only one thing—to keep daylight between them and their pursuers until night fell. They still had a long time to go.

Indy heard Herman gasping behind him. "Hey, Indy, got to catch my breath."

Indy stopped and stood with his back pressed against a rock. Herman did the same beside him.

"Say, that was real nice of the old woman," Herman said, as he sucked air into his lungs. "I mean, she didn't know us at all."

"These people have a great custom of kindness to travelers," Indy said. "I guess she decided to treat us as her guests. Even though we were uninvited."

"Pretty lucky she had that back door," said Herman. "Otherwise, we'd be guests of King Zed and Count Igor again. And I can do without *their* kindness to guests."

"I doubt it was luck," Indy said. "People around here have had to deal with invaders, bandits, tax collectors, and other bad guys for thousands of years. They want to be able to get out of a place fast."

"Well, I want to get out of *this* place fast," said Herman. "That whip of yours isn't going to do much good against those rifles. Say, where did you get that whip, anyway?"

"Off a sleeping camel driver. When we

rested at midday yesterday," said Indy. "A whip can come in real handy in tight spots." He took out the camel driver's whip and looked at it. He shook his head. "This isn't near as good as the bullwhip I've got at home. I've been practicing how to use it. It's amazing what it can do. I should have taken it along, but I didn't. I won't make that mistake again."

"Yeah, don't leave home without it," said Herman. "Hey, that's a pretty catchy phrase, huh? Bet you could sell a lot of bullwhips with it."

"Or sell something," said Indy. "You should go into advertising when you grow up."

"*If* I grow up," said Herman, as a rifle shot cracked in the air. There was a puff of dust as a bullet hit the ground near their feet.

Indy looked up at where the shot came from. One of King Zed's men stood on top of a rock. He had a smoking rifle in his hands.

"Let's move it," said Indy. "Keep close to the rock, so he can't get a clear shot at us."

They made it around the rock. But on the

other side they saw something alarming. Other armed men. In gaps between the rocks, and on top of rocks.

"They've fanned out all around us," Indy said.

"Yeah," said Herman, panting. "We're being hunted down like rabbits."

"Wish we were as fast as rabbits," said Indy. Then his mouth dropped open. "Hey, speaking of rabbits, see what I see?"

Scared by the shooting, a large gray hare went tearing past them. It headed straight for a cluster of bushes and disappeared into them.

"We can be as smart as a rabbit, anyway," said Indy. "Those bushes will have to do as a hiding place. They're the best place I can see right now."

The boys dashed for the bushes. "Hope those other guys haven't spotted us yet," Herman panted.

"Sorry, rabbit, you've got company," said Indy. He and Herman got down on their hands and knees and crawled into the shrubbery.

But the hare wasn't there.

"Must have chased him away," muttered Indy. Then he said, "Herman, look. *This* is what the rabbit was heading for."

Hidden by the bushes was a slanting hole in the ground.

"But this wasn't made by any rabbit," said Herman. "It's big enough for a person."

"Right," said Indy. "The rabbit just knew it was here. It must be another escape route that the people around here built. Probably leads to a underground chamber. Some kind of temporary hideout to use until the heat is off." He grinned. "Well, what are we waiting for?"

"Go down *there*?" said Herman. "It's kind of dark and creepy. Besides, who knows what's down there. Rats. Snakes."

Indy turned pale and slightly green. "*Snakes?* I hadn't thought of that."

"Sure," said Herman. "It's a natural place for them to live. Wonder if they have rattlers in Turkey. Or maybe cobras. Or asps."

"Look, let's change the subject, okay?" said Indy. He swallowed hard.

Just then there was the sound of shouting men coming closer.

"They'll be beating the bushes in a couple of minutes," said Indy. "It's either this hole— or an early grave."

"Well, if you put it *that* way," said Herman. "But since it's your idea, you go first."

"Yeah, okay, okay," said Indy. But he was in no rush. "Hey, Herman," he said, as he tried to make himself go into the hole. "You ever read *Alice in Wonderland*?"

"No. Why?" said Herman. He never stopped being amazed at what was in Indy's head. And at what popped out of his mouth.

"It's about this girl who follows a rabbit down a hole," Indy said.

"So what happens to her?" asked Herman. But as Indy was opening his mouth to answer, Herman said, "Don't bother telling me. I'm more interested in what happens to *us*. Those guys are almost here."

"We'll find out soon enough," said Indy. He swallowed hard again. And took a deep breath. No more stalling. "Wonderland, here we come."

# Chapter 9

"Indy, I've got a funny feeling about this," Herman said.

They had already left daylight far behind. The slanting hole in the ground turned out to be far deeper than they had imagined. And far darker. But stone steps made it easy for the boys to go down. They used their hands as well as their feet, the same way they would go down a ladder.

"Funny feeling?" said Indy. "What kind of funny feeling?"

Actually, he had a funny feeling himself.

Or rather, a not so funny feeling. It was a feeling that made him shiver. A feeling that any moment he would hear a snake's angry hiss. Or feel a snake's slimy body coil around him. Or have a snake's fangs sink into his flesh. Snakes. Brrr.

Indy couldn't shake off that chilling fear, try as he might. He had a thing about snakes, and that was that. The best he could do was keep his fear out of his voice. He didn't want to give Herman anything else to be afraid of. Herman was scared enough as it was. And they'd never get out of this jam if Herman turned totally afraid.

"I've got a feeling that we've done all this before," Herman said. "In fact, it's more than a feeling. It's a fact. Remember when we went down those steps to reach that underground passageway back in Konya? We walked right into trouble. I have a feeling we're walking into trouble again. Except the trouble is even deeper this time."

"Come on, let's not slow down," Indy said. He kept up the pace going down the steps, with Herman right above him. "This is no time to panic. This is nothing like Konya. *That* time we were following that King Zed guy. *This* time *he*'s after *us*. We're not getting *into* trouble, we're getting *out* of it. And there's no trap door to fall down over the hole. We can always go back out the way we came in. The whole thing is completely different."

"Okay, okay, it *is* different," Herman admitted. "But I have this other feeling, too."

Indy sighed. He was still moving downward as fast as he could. "What's this other feeling?"

"That King Zed guy. He seemed right at home underground," Herman said. "Like it was the only place he could take off his wraps and play king. I've got a feeling we're in his territory, not ours. It's like we're playing a game on his home field."

"And I thought *I* was the one with a wild imagination," Indy said. "You should write adventure stories, Herman. Or at least not read so many of them."

Indy then closed the discussion. "You should be grateful for these steps, not scared of them," he stated firmly. "Whoever built this hole got us out of the hole we were in. *That* hole could have become our grave."

"Yeah, well, *this* hole is going a whole lot deeper than any grave," Herman said. "It feels like we've been going down it forever."

"It probably leads to some real safe hiding place," said Indy. "Or maybe it goes upward at some point to a secret exit. Either way, we just have to stay underground until it's night. Then we can go out without Zed and his men spotting us. After that, we're practically home free. Just keep watching your step. I don't want you to come crashing down on top of me."

Indy followed his own advice. He carefully checked out each step with his foot before he put his weight on it. This was what it must feel like to be blind, he thought. Moving through pitch-darkness with only your sense of touch to guide you. It was scary and exciting at the same time, the way the unknown always was.

Then he noticed something even more scary and exciting. He could dimly make out his hands in front of him.

He looked downward.

Light was coming from below.

Far below he could see the steps ending in a lit doorway.

He heard Herman's voice from above him. "Indy, you see what I see? I got a funny—"

"Don't say it," Indy said. "Some people live down here, that's all. If the local natives live in rocks, they can just as easily live in holes."

"Yeah, sure," said Herman. He didn't sound convinced. "But I bet they might be kind of annoyed if we barge in uninvited."

"They won't mind," Indy assured him. "You've already seen how friendly these people are to strangers. We can depend on that Turkish kindness. Why, they'll probably even help us find the fastest way to get back to Konya."

The boys reached the entranceway and went through it. They found themselves in a tunnel carved through the soft rock. The tunnel was lit by oil lamps in holes along its sides. Looking down the tunnel, the boys could also see doorways on both sides.

"This is wild," said Indy, as they moved along the passageway. He could see rooms through the doorways. Rooms complete with furniture and carpets!

Finally the passageway branched off in two directions. "Which way now?" Indy wondered. He swiveled his gaze right and left. There were more lit lamps and doorways in both directions.

"There's a whole maze of rooms down here," he said. "We've stumbled onto something big."

"Look, mazes are what people get *lost* in," Herman said. "Let's go back the way we came, while we still can find it."

But Indy wasn't listening. He was too busy trying to figure out something.

"The air down here is good," he mused. "I can't even smell smoke from the lamps. It must be drawn away somewhere. There has to be some kind of fresh air system."

He headed down the passageway to his right. And soon found what he was looking for. At the end of the passageway was a large, well-like hole in the rock floor. Right above it was a similar hole in the ceiling. Indy held out his hand. He felt a breeze.

"An air shaft," he said. "It must go all the

way up to the surface. I wonder how far down it goes." He picked up a stone and dropped it into the hole. He waited. There was no sound of it hitting bottom.

"There must be more levels of rooms below," Indy went on. "A lot more. Who could have built all this? It would take an army of workers."

"Indy?" said Herman behind him.

Indy didn't bother turning around. "We'll find a way down to the next level, that's all," he said. "Then we'll head back up, I promise."

"*Indy,*" Herman said more urgently.

"*What?*" said Indy impatiently, as he tried to think of where a way down might be.

"Tell me about Turkish kindness again," Herman said.

Indy turned to follow Herman's frozen stare. A man was blocking the passageway down which they had come. He was dressed in old-fashioned robes. But he was holding a modern rifle. And it was pointed straight at them.

# Chapter 10

The man spoke no English. But he didn't need to use his tongue. He moved the barrel of his gun to tell the boys where he wanted them to go.

He herded them through the maze of passageways. At last they reached a flight of steps. They went down to a lower level of passageways and rooms. Then down more steps to a still lower level.

Indy kept his eyes open, taking in everything. They passed people now—men, women, and children. They passed kitchens and dining halls and rooms with beds. Indy spotted large boulders that could be rolled to block off the ends of passageways in case of attack. He checked out the guards at the head of each set of steps. They were armed to the teeth, with modern rifles and pistols. And with old-fashioned swords and daggers.

"It's a fortress," Indy said to Herman. "They can keep anybody they want from getting into here."

"Or out of here," said Herman glumly.

"Looks like we're coming to something," said Indy. They had reached a level with larger passageways. The walls and floors and roofs were not rough rock. Instead, there were beautiful tiles in bright patterns.

"Yeah, we're coming to something," agreed Herman. The rifle poked him in the back. "And it feels like the end of the line."

"Wow," said Indy, as they turned a corner. They stood in a hall leading to a huge golden double door. Two guards stood in front of the door. They were dressed like ancient warriors, with golden breastplates.

They carried golden shields and long spears with blades of gold.

The man with the rifle spoke to the guards. They swung the great door open.

The rifle prodded the boys through the doorway.

"I don't believe it," said Indy.

"You and me both," said Herman.

The room was vast, and blazing with torchlight. A great golden throne stood in its center.

From the throne a voice boomed down. "So you finally arrived. What took you so long?"

"The king," gasped Herman.

"I guess he really is one," Indy said to Herman out of the side of his mouth. Indy's gaze took in Zed's throne. His jeweled crown. And the scepter that he held. Indy felt a chill when he saw the symbol on that scepter. A bone-white death's head.

Then Indy added, "And the count's real, too."

Count Igor stood to the right of the throne. He wore a splendidly cut forest-green uniform. A high black fur hussar's hat was on his head. Medals and ribbons covered his chest. An ermine-trimmed cavalry cape was thrown over his shoulders. Richly gleaming black boots rose to his knees.

"The king was right," the count said, smiling. "Our men reported you had stumbled on one of our entrances. The king said you'd find your way down here."

"I knew what curious boys you are," the king said. He was smiling, too. His smile was both happy and cruel. Indy would have bet that when the king was a kid, he picked wings off flies to watch them wiggle.

"I knew we shouldn't have gone down that hole," Herman muttered to Indy. "I told you so."

But Indy was far more interested in what the king had to say.

"I ordered men to guard the hole so you couldn't get back out," the king went on. "Then I told my men down here to wait for you to arrive."

"So now you've got us where you want us," said Indy.

"But don't you want to know what I want you for?" the king asked.

"I didn't think I had to ask," Indy said. "I can see that you're dying to tell us."

The king gave a royal chuckle. "It is not I who will be doing the dying."

"Ha ha," said Indy sarcastically.

Herman tapped him on the arm. "Look, Indy, maybe you should take it easy. No sense getting His Majesty mad," he whispered.

"Mad?" said Indy as loudly as he could. "He already is. Insane, I mean. Delusions of grandeur. First calling himself King of Kings. Then this stuff about killing us. When all he's really after is ransom money from my dad. Everybody thinks all Americans are rich. This guy is out for a few bucks. He's just a cheap crook."

"Indy, what are you *doing*?" said Herman with horror, as he watched the king's face darken with rage.

Indy, though, knew exactly what he was doing. He wanted to wipe the smile off the king's face. He wanted to end the game of cat and mouse the king was playing. He wanted the king to show his teeth—and his hand. The more Indy knew about the king's plans, and the faster he knew it, the better it would be. He would have more chances of dodging the threat hanging over Herman and him like a sword.

"Enough talk," Zed thundered. "I will show you what the King of Kings can do."

He clapped his hands once. It echoed in the vast room like a rifle shot.

Two men entered—on their hands and knees. They crawled to the throne and threw themselves facedown.

The king said, "Rise," and they obeyed. "We will speak in English so these boys will understand who I am and what they must do. That is why I have made you learn English and all the other languages of those who rule the world today. That is why I learned them. So that the rulers of the world will understand me when I tell them what to do."

"Yes, O King of Kings," the two men said together, as they stood up.

They were an odd pair. One was thin as a needle, with sharp features to match. The other was immensely fat. He had a round body and a bowling ball of a hairless head.

"First, have you made sure that the date is correct?" the king asked the thin man.

"For all my life, I have been studying the sacred tablets," the man said. "For the past year, I have been studying the stars through our new telescope."

"Given by the czar, if I may remind you, Your Majesty," the count said.

"Yes, yes, I will remember that," the king said impatiently. Then he said to the thin man, "I asked you a simple question. Are you sure of the right date?"

"I will stake my life on it," the man declared.

"You *are* staking your life on it," the king said. Then he asked the fat man, "Are you ready to do your work?"

"Of course, O King of Kings," the fat man said. "I need only fetch my instruments."

"Then get them, and get on with it," the king commanded.

It was the fat man's turn to clap his hands.

Two servants entered the room. One carried an instrument case made of gold. The other carried a golden tray. On the tray was a dull white stone the shape of an egg.

"Now we need only one more thing," the fat man said.

"Tell the boys what it is," the king said. "I know how curious they are."

The fat man turned to Herman and Indy. "Your blood," he said.

# Chapter 11

"This won't hurt a bit," the fat man said, as he opened his instrument case.

"Last time I heard that was from a dentist," Herman said. "He lied."

Indy gave Herman a look that said, *Don't let them see that you're afraid.*

Herman answered with a look that clearly declared, *But I* am *afraid.*

All Indy could do was say, "I'll go first." He stepped forward to stand before the fat man.

The fat man opened his instrument case. He took out a long silver needle.

"Give me your hand," he commanded.

Indy swallowed hard and extended his hand. The fat man seized it by the wrist. In a swift, expert motion he stuck the needle into Indy's thumb.

Indy didn't give the fat man the satisfaction of hearing him say ouch. He didn't even blink at the sharp pain. He bit his lower lip and kept his gaze steady. He watched the fat man squeeze drops of blood out of the pricked thumb. The blood dripped onto the egg-shaped white stone.

The stone began to glow. It was as if a light had been turned on inside it.

"Good!" the fat man exclaimed. "Now for the other one."

The blood was washed from the stone, and the glow faded.

"Now the other boy," the king commanded.

"Ouch!" shouted Herman at the top of his lungs, as his blood was taken and tested.

"Excellent!" the fat man said, as the stone glowed again. He bowed to King Zed. "O King of Kings, the sacred stone that never

lies has told the truth. Both boys are innocent. You can use either one you choose."

"Hmmm," the king said. "That is a problem. Which one do I want? I'll make up my
mind later. There is still time." He turned
to the thin man. "How much time is there?"

The thin man pulled out a gold pocket
watch and squinted at it.

"Exactly ten hours and four minutes to the
stroke of midnight," he said.

"You mean we have to wait that long to
find out what this nonsense is all about?"
Indy said. "Come on. Give us a break."

"Ten hours is not so long," the king told
him. "My family has waited for this moment for almost four thousand years."

"Sure. Right. Four thousand years," Indy
mocked. "You can't fool us. You're not only
a kidnaper. You're a con man, too. All that
phony mumbo jumbo with that idol in
Konya. And now *this* mumbo jumbo. Come
on, 'fess up. We know you're no more a king
than you were a dervish."

But the king refused to get angry. He
smiled. "Your talk does not bother me. It is

no more than the buzzing of a tiny fly. A fly that I can easily squash. But I, Zed, King of Kings, will be merciful. I will give meaning to your miserable little lives. I will let you know why you will die."

"Sure, tell us," said Indy. "It should be at least good for a laugh."

"We will see who has the last laugh," the king said. "Come midnight, my triumphant laughter will ring out over all the land."

"Okay, okay. Enough build-up," said Indy, still needling as hard as he could. "Get on with your fairy tale."

"Do you know the Old Testament of the Bible?" the king asked. "Do you think that is a fairy tale?"

"I know the Bible," Indy said. "Anybody who wants to know about history has to."

"Then you know the story of Cain and Abel," said the king.

"Sure," said Indy. "They were brothers. The sons of Adam and Eve. Cain got mad at Abel and killed him. He was the first killer."

"Very good," said the king. "I see you are a young scholar. But do you know what happened to Cain after the killing?"

Indy thought a moment. "He was banished from his family home. He had to go live east of Eden. In the land of Nod." Indy paused, then went on. "There's something else, too. He was branded by the Lord for his crime. With some kind of mark. The mark of Cain."

"And what was that mark?" the king asked.

"I don't think the Bible says," said Indy. "Actually, I'm sure it doesn't."

"You're right," the king said. "It is not in the Bible. At least, not in the Bible *you* know. But there is another Bible that tells another story."

"I've heard of it," Indy said. "It's called the Apocrypha. A collection of weird legends and superstitions. Different versions have popped up all over the world."

"But there is only one true version," the king said. His voice had deepened, as if his words came from the bottom of his soul. "*That* version tells how the Lord of Darkness gave Cain a knife. He gave Cain a promise, as well. With that knife Cain would be granted safety from all harm. And power over all he wished to rule."

The king lowered his voice even more. "All Cain had to do for this was dip the knife in Abel's blood and introduce murder to the world. After that, the power of the knife would belong to Cain. It would pass to those who possessed the knife after him, down through time to the end of time."

Indy shook his head. "I have to hand it to you, King. You've got a royal imagination."

"You don't believe me?" the king demanded.

"The story has too many holes," said Indy, shrugging. "For one thing, Cain sure didn't get what he bargained for. I mean, after he killed Abel, your Lord of Darkness left him high and dry."

"Not at all," the king insisted. "Cain went to Nod, as *your* Bible says. But what it does not say is that he became its ruler. No man could kill him, no enemy defeat him."

"But there was a catch, right?" said Indy, playing along with this crazy tale. "I mean, his rule over Nod didn't last."

"Yes, there was a 'catch,' as you call it," the king admitted. "The power of the knife lasted only as long as Cain lived out his natural life. One hundred years. After that, his empire fell, and his heirs had to flee."

"So it was a trick, that talk about being able to hand down his knife," said Indy. "He could hand it down, but it would be worthless."

"It was no trick," said the king. "It was the never-ending wisdom of the Lord of Darkness. He wanted to make sure that the spirit of murder never vanished from the earth. That there would always be those who worshiped its memory. And prayed for its return."

"Tricky guy, that Lord of Darkness," Indy said, shaking his head. Did the king really expect him to believe all this? The trouble was, the king seemed to believe it. And that was bad news. Very bad news.

Meanwhile, the king went on, his voice growing even stronger. "So the Lord of Darkness declared that when the stars and planets and moon were in the same position as they were when Abel was killed, the knife's power would return. And it would last the same length of time that Cain enjoyed it. One hundred years. But to gain that power one had to do what Cain did. Dip that knife in blood." The king paused and smiled at the boys, his pointed teeth gleaming. "Innocent blood."

Indy tried to keep mocking. "You actually expect us to believe that?"

"Do you believe this?" the king demanded.

From a jeweled sheath he drew out a knife. It was made of crude iron and was very old.

"And this?" He parted his royal robes to expose his naked chest.

On his chest was a huge red birthmark.

"No, don't tell me that's—" Indy gasped.

"*Yes,*" the king said. "The mark of Cain."

# Chapter 12

"Do you believe me now?" the king asked. He put the knife back in its sheath and covered his chest again.

Indy made one more try at an argument.

"So you have that mark. So what?" he said. "That doesn't mean all the rest of that stuff is true. About the magic power of the knife. About dipping it in . . ." Indy paused and gulped. "Dipping it in innocent blood. Supposing that isn't true. I mean, it's never been tried. And then you'd lose the ransom money you could get for us."

"But it *has* been tried," the king said.

"When?" asked Indy.

"Once before, three thousand years ago, the time was right," the king said. "My ancestor performed the sacred rite of blood. The power of the knife was his for a hundred years."

"Yeah?" said Indy. "Then why haven't we heard of him? What did he do with all that so-called power?"

"First he conquered a huge empire," said the king. "It took him only twenty years. Then he prepared for when the power of the knife would fade. Millions of slaves worked fifty years to build a great city. A city where he could lead his people when he could no longer defend his empire. *An underground city.*"

The king made a gesture that took in the throne room they were in. And all the other rooms and passageways and stairways Indy had seen. And all the ones Indy could only imagine. Indy shook his head in awe at how immense this place must be.

"There were sources of water here," the king went on. "And many, many rooms to store food. Passages could be blocked off so no enemies could get through. And so, when the mighty Hittites swept down from the north, he led his people underground. Here his royal descendants could wait until the power of the knife was theirs again."

"You mean people have been living down here for *three thousand years*?" Indy said.

"I am the living proof of that," the king said, drawing himself up proudly. "Above ground, the Hittites destroyed all traces of our empire. But down here, we survived. Fewer and fewer of us, but we did it."

"And no one ever found you?" said Indy.

"In all those years?" said Herman, shaking his head.

"The first ones who found us, we killed," the king said with a shrug. "Then, when there were too many of them, we retreated. We left the upper levels of our city to other hunted people. Christians fleeing pagans. Pagans fleeing Christians. Christians fleeing Islam. To get around them, we built separate entrances to the lower levels we live in now."

"Entrances like the one we stumbled onto," said Indy.

"Yeah, lucky us," said Herman.

The king ignored them. He was deep into his story now. He was reliving the deeds of his ancestors. "We used those secret entrances to go to the surface and farm for food. We also used them to send people all over the land. Those people kept in touch with what was going on. We had to be ready when our day in the sun came again."

"Those people you were dancing in front of in Konya," said Indy. "They were spies from your underground kingdom."

The king nodded. "My loyal servants. Loyal as my people have always been, for three thousand years. Above ground, they had to pretend first to be Christian, then Islamic. But all the while they kept the faith. The only true faith. Faith in the power of darkness. Faith in the coming of the time of Cain. A hundred years when killing will be king. Now at last, the stars and sun and moon are right again. Tonight at the stroke of midnight, that century begins."

Indy thought quickly. "That's June 28."

"Yes, by your calendar," the king said. "You can mark that date in red. *June 28, 1914.*" He smiled. Indy could tell the king was looking forward to midnight.

"It will begin the most terrifying hundred years in history," the king said. "And you will have the honor of being the first of its millions and millions of victims."

"But don't any of your people want the honor?" asked Indy.

"Yeah, I mean, they have dibs," said Herman.

"There is no innocent blood among *my* people," the king said proudly. "As I told you, they have kept the faith. We were going to use a local villager—but then you came along. The shedding of American blood will cause less hard feeling than Turkish blood."

"This can't be happening," Herman said. "I mean, this is the twentieth century."

"Ask your friend if this is happening," the king suggested.

Herman turned to Indy. He waited for Indy to tell him to relax. And not to worry.

Indy was silent.

Then Herman saw something that made him go limp with relief. Indy gave him a wink. A quick one, so that only he would see it. But it was enough to tell Herman that Indy had a plan.

And that was enough for Herman. Indy had gotten out of tight spots before. Indy would do it again.

Herman was eager to find out from Indy what the plan was. But when the king sent them off to wait for midnight, he sent English-speaking guards with them. Those guards stayed too close for Indy to say anything.

It was only later, much later, that Herman had his chance to ask.

They stood off by themselves in a vast underground temple. In it was a statue like the one they had seen in Konya. A monstrous figure of a man holding a blood-red knife. But this statue was ten times larger.

The king stood on a raised platform in front of the huge idol. Next to him was a golden basin. In his hand was the Knife of Cain. And in front of him the temple was packed with spellbound people. Everyone in the underground kingdom must have gathered for this moment.

Count Igor approached the king with a large cloth sack. That was when Herman saw his chance. All eyes turned to the count as he poured a stream of gold coins at the idol's feet. Herman hurriedly whispered to Indy, "Okay, what's the plan?"

"What plan?" Indy whispered back.

"Your plan," Herman whispered impatiently. Sometimes Indy's sense of humor drove him crazy. "The escape plan. The one you gave me that wink about."

Indy looked uncomfortable. "Uhhh, Herman, that wasn't exactly a wink. A speck of dust got in my eye."

"You mean . . . ?" Herman said.

Indy nodded bleakly.

Just then a man came to stand by their side.

"I am your interpreter," he said. He smiled unpleasantly at them. "His Majesty wishes that you understand everything that is being said. He says he will enjoy watching your faces as your fate becomes clearer and clearer."

From the platform the king made a ringing statement.

The interpreter gave an instant translation.

"Now is the time for the final offering to the Lord of Darkness. The gift of blood."

# Chapter 13

"If only we had more time," Herman said helplessly.

"We've got a bit of time," Indy replied. "There are always long speeches at big events like this. Count on it."

Indy was right. The speeches went on and on. The interpreter grew hoarse as he translated them.

First the king spoke. He told of the great day about to dawn. All over Turkey his people were ready and waiting. As soon as the king showed himself above ground, they would take over the government. The Knife of Cain would take care of anyone who dared oppose them. But perhaps the knife would not even be needed. They had more than enough money in their war chest. They also had a great warehouse of the most modern weapons. For this the king thanked Count Igor.

Count Igor spoke next. He promised the eternal friendship of the Russian czar. He was sure that Russia and the new Turkish empire under King Zed would be strong enough to rule the world between them. And he gave thanks to King Zed. The king had promised that Russian ships could use the Dardanelles waterway to reach and control the Mediterranean.

Count Igor was still spouting promises when a man in white robes urgently tugged at King Zed's sleeve. The man pulled out a pocket watch and pointed to it. King Zed nodded. Then he stepped in front of the count, cutting him off in mid-sentence.

"The stroke of midnight is fast approaching," the king announced. "Let the ceremony begin. Bring the two innocents up here."

Herman threw Indy a desperate look. Had Indy come up with a plan?

Indy did not look at Herman. All he could say was "Showdown time, I guess."

Guards hustled Herman and Indy up onto the platform. The two boys stood before King Zed. The Knife of Cain was in the king's hand. And Indy and Herman didn't have to be told what the golden basin by his side was for.

The king spoke to them in English. He seemed to be feasting on their fear.

"There is only one question now before the prayers of three thousand years are answered," the king said. "Which of you two boys should have the supreme joy of the Knife of Cain cutting your vein? Whose blood will turn the knife blood-red for the next hundred glorious years?"

Indy cleared his throat. "I hate to be a tattletale," he said. "But my pal Herman here, he's not as innocent as he looks. There was the time I caught him smoking corn silk behind the barn. And I'm pretty sure he didn't tie all the knots for his Boy Scout merit badge. Plus, I once spotted him looking over my shoulder in a geography quiz. No, Herman is definitely not your boy. Now take me, on the other hand. The sweetest, gentlest, most innocent kid you could ever hope to find."

King Zed looked hard at Indy. He licked his lips. "I have been wanting to wipe that insulting smile off your face, my young American. Now I will."

"Okay, I'll take my medicine," Indy said. He gritted his teeth, and stepped forward. At least Herman would still have a chance to survive. Not much of one. But better than nothing.

King Zed held up his hand to stop Indy. The king chuckled. "Killing you now would let you off too easy. I want to see your face when you watch your friend die. I want to see you make jokes about that."

The king rubbed his hands together and went on. "After that, of course, it will be your turn. But I'll need some time to think how I will kill you. I'll want it to be as slow and painful as possible."

"Sorry, Herman, I tried," Indy said in a broken voice.

"I know you did, Indy," Herman managed to choke out of his dry throat. "Nice try, anyway."

The king gave a nod. A guard used a spear to prod Herman to the basin. Another guard held Herman's wrist over it. The wrist was turned upward. Indy could see the blue vein with Herman's blood pulsing through it. The king looked at it carefully. Then he raised the knife.

*"Here goes—everything,"* Indy said to himself, and reached into his robe.

A heartbeat later, the camel driver's whip was in his hand.

Before anyone could stop him, he sent the lash curling around the king's knife hand.

The king's howl of pain echoed through the temple. And the knife went flying through the air.

Everyone froze.

Everyone but Indy.

As the knife hit the stone platform with a clatter, Indy dove after it.

Then everyone else moved at once, going for it too.

Indy's head start won him the prize. His hand closed over the hilt. Holding the knife in front of him, he got to his feet.

The king thundered a command to his guards.

But none of them moved. Terror was in their eyes as they stared at the knife in Indy's hand.

"Then I'll get it myself," King Zed snarled at Indy.

He grabbed a sword from a guard and moved toward Indy with it poised to slash.

Indy saw only one play to make.

"Here, Herman, catch!" he yelled. And tossed the knife, hilt first, to Herman.

Indy shuddered as he did so. He remembered all the passes he had thrown to Herman in sandlot football games. He couldn't remember Herman ever catching one.

"Attaboy, Herman!" Indy shouted with

relief, as he saw Herman's hand grab at the hilt and hold on to it.

Herman looked more surprised than Indy.

He stared at the knife and shook his head. *What was he supposed to do with it?*

King Zed, though, knew what to do. Sword in hand, he turned toward Herman and charged.

Herman waited a split second, then grinned.

"Indy, catch!" he shouted, and let the knife fly.

But this time the king was ready. He leapt into the air, his free hand reaching high. He would have made a great defenseman. He caught the knife for a perfect interception.

And all Indy could think was, there goes the old ball game.

# Chapter 14

Indy was ready for King Zed's shout of joy.

But instead, he heard King Zed scream.

Then Indy saw what had happened.

The king had caught the knife by the blade instead of the hilt. And from the look of fear on his face, he must have known what would happen when that blade cut his hand.

That fear spread instantly to everyone who watched—Indy, Herman, Count Igor, and all the king's people.

The king's scream of pain lasted only a moment. Then the scream died with the king.

It was as if an invisible fire was burning his body. His clothes shriveled. His flesh melted. His bones were eaten away. Within minutes, he was a small heap of black ashes.

The knife lay on the platform beside the ashes. Its metallic-colored blade had not turned red. It was now jet-black.

Wrong type of blood, Indy thought. Definitely not innocent.

That was as far as his thinking went.

A hand swooped down and scooped up the knife.

The count's hand.

The count's other hand grabbed Herman.

Then the count yelled to Indy, "Come on! *Run!* While there's still time."

Indy's mouth dropped open. But he didn't have time to wonder what the count was doing. And he couldn't argue with what the count had said. This was the time to make a break for it.

For the moment, the king's people were in shock. The sound of their moaning and wailing filled the vast room. But when they recovered, they would want revenge.

"He's right!" Indy shouted to Herman, who was being unwillingly dragged along. "Let's make tracks!"

Herman nodded and started matching the count's running steps. Indy kept up with them as they raced out of the room.

Outside, the passageways and rooms were deserted. Everyone *had* gone to watch the ceremony.

"Where are we going?" gasped Herman, as they ran through one passageway into another and into another after that.

"Only one way to go," said Indy. "Up."

"Here's a stairway," said the count.

They took it two stone steps at a time.

At the top was an oil lamp. Beyond its flickering flame was darkness.

"This is where the king's hideout ends," said Indy. "The empty levels of the underground city must be above us."

"Hey, before we go any farther, I want to know what *you're* doing here," Herman said to the count.

"With the king dead, I'm in as much danger as you are," the count said. "As far as his people are concerned, all outsiders are the same. Now outsiders have killed their king. So they'll want outsiders' lives in return, as many as they can take. We have to stick together and help each other."

He saw the doubt in Herman's eyes and went on. "You'll find out something as you grow up. People who don't much like each other can become partners when their lives are at stake."

"I feel like I'm growing up pretty fast right now," said Herman.

"I hope we both get a chance to grow up some more," said Indy. "But we won't unless we find a way out of here."

The count nodded. "Unfortunately, the king said all connections to the upper levels are blocked off."

"Never hurts to see for yourself," said Indy. He took the lamp and led the way into the darkness.

"Brave boy," the count said approvingly.

"That's Indy," Herman agreed.

They moved through the passageway until they hit a stone wall. A passageway branching off led to another dead end.

"We'll have to go back down," said the

count. "Maybe I can make some kind of deal."

"I wouldn't count on it, Count," said Indy. "Let's make one more try."

They went down another passageway.

"Touchdown!" said Indy.

There was a hole in the stone wall.

"Maybe an earthquake caused it," Indy said. "It's just big enough to squeeze through."

"Big enough for you to squeeze through," said the count. "Not me."

"Look, I'll go through and see what's there," said Indy.

"And abandon me here?" the count said.

"I wouldn't do that to anyone, not even *you*," said Indy.

"You can trust Indy," said Herman.

"*You'll* have to trust him, too—with your life," the count said. He took a firm hold on Herman's arm and said to Indy, "Go ahead."

Indy squeezed through the hole. The count passed the oil lamp through to him. Then the count and Herman waited in the pitch-darkness. And waited. And waited.

"See how foolish you were to trust him,"

the count said. His grip tightened on Herman's arm. "That is the first rule of survival. Never trust anyone."

"Maybe he got lost," Herman suggested. "Maybe—"

"Maybe I will take you back downstairs," said the count. "Maybe I will offer you as a peace offering to the people there. I don't think it will work, but it's better than nothing."

*"No,"* Herman protested as the count started to drag him away. "Just wait a—"

"Hey, good news!" Indy's voice never sounded sweeter. "I found some old tools. We can make the hole bigger."

The light from the oil lamp lit the hole. Indy passed an old pickax through it. The count grabbed it in his huge hands and started swinging. From the other side came the noise of Indy doing the same.

In less than half an hour, the count made it through the hole. Herman followed him.

"Thank you, young man," the count said to Indy. "I owe you my life." Then he smiled. "And soon I will owe you even more."

With that, he grabbed Herman again with

one hand. And with the other he pulled out the blackened knife.

"What are you doing?" cried Herman.

"As I already told you," the count sneered, "you must trust no one. And let me add now, *especially not me.*"

# Chapter 15

The truth dawned on Indy. He blinked and shook his head. He could not believe it.

"You don't mean to use the knife?" he asked the count. "Why, that's crazy."

"That's what I thought, at first," the count said. He kept a tight grip on Herman. "I thought Zed was a madman. It didn't matter to me. Madmen have overthrown governments before. And if he succeeded, Turkey would be Russia's partner. If war ever breaks out in Europe, that will be very important."

"Sure, that makes sense," said Indy. "But this stuff with the knife. It's nonsense."

"You say that—after you saw what the knife did to the king?" the count said.

Indy couldn't say anything to that. He could only note the gleam in the count's eyes. The same gleam he had seen in the king's eyes. The gleam of insane ambition.

"The knife does have power—the power the king claimed," the count declared. "My country, too, is ready for revolution. The czar is weak and foolish. The people are angry and eager for change. With this knife I can take over. And with this knife in my hand and Russia behind me I can rule the world."

Indy tried a different argument. "Look at that knife. Black as tar. It's ruined."

"Nothing that innocent blood won't fix," the count said. "Especially if I give it a double dose to make sure."

Indy made one last try. "The right time has gone by. The stroke of midnight has passed. You've missed the boat."

"You didn't listen to the king closely enough," the count said. "The stroke of midnight merely marked the start of the century. The century when the knife has the power of supreme rule. Zed didn't want to miss a minute of it. That power is still waiting to be turned on. And now it is in my hands."

Enough words, thought Indy.

He pulled out his whip and sent its lash toward the count's knife hand.

The count answered with a laugh, as the knife neatly sliced the lash in two.

"You wanted to use your little toy against *this*?" he sneered. "Now is the time to say your prayers—to the Lord of Darkness. The time to bow to the power of the knife."

"You're wrong," said Indy. "Now is the time for *this*!"

Swiftly he scooped up a rock and fired a high hard one at the count's head.

Laughing, the count held up the knife and let the rock bounce off it.

He opened his mouth to make another remark. But what came out was *"Agghhhh!"*

Indy hadn't paused after he threw the rock. He had picked up the oil lamp from the floor and flung it in the count's face.

Just before the lamp went out, Indy saw

the count let go of Herman to put his hand to his burned cheek.

Indy reached out in the dark and found Herman's robe.

"The old one-two punch. Never fails," Indy said. "Let's go. Take hold of my robe so we stay together."

Indy led the way, running down the pitch-dark passageway. It had to lead somewhere. Indy hoped it wasn't to a dead end.

Behind him he heard the count's running footsteps, too. For a man so huge, the count moved fast. He was gaining.

Then Indy felt something on his face. A very slight breeze. He desperately skidded to a halt. Sticking out his arm, he stopped Herman and grabbed him. He forced Herman to press beside him against the passageway wall.

Then he shouted loudly. "Come on, Herman! Move it! I see a way out up ahead!"

A few moments later, the count's footsteps pounded past them. The next second, that sound was replaced by a scream. A scream that swiftly faded. Then silence. Dead silence.

"There was an air shaft ahead of us," Indy explained to Herman. "From the sound of that scream, it must go really far down. To the king's hideout. Maybe even farther."

"That takes care of the count. And the knife," said Herman. "That just leaves one little thing to take care of. *Us*. We still have to get out of here."

"No problem," said Indy. "They must have built this underground city in some kind of pattern. We have to figure out how the passageways and stairways are arranged. Then we can go up level by level to the surface. It'll be easy."

Hours later, the boys were caked with dust and soaked in sweat. But the dirt and the sweat were forgotten when they saw light ahead. Indy stood on tiptoes, gripped the edge of a hole in the ground above them, and lifted himself out.

Then he reached down and helped Herman climb out, too.

"Whew," said Herman. "If that was easy, I don't want to know what hard is."

"No sweat now, though," said Indy. "From here on, it's all downhill."

"Sure," said Herman. He looked around him at the rock fantasy world of Cappadocia. The dawn was turning the eastern sky pink. "Now all we have to do is find a way to get back to Konya."

"First things first," said Indy. He was scanning the landscape, looking for a certain rock formation.

"There it is," he said, spotting the rock he remembered.

He led Herman to it. Near its base was the hole leading to Zed's hideout.

"Come on. We've got work to do," he said, putting his shoulder to a large boulder. Together they rolled it over the hole.

"I get you," Herman said, nodding. "This will slow down Zed's people when they come after us. They'll have to back up and use another way to get out."

"There's a more important reason," Indy said. "It'll help keep anyone from finding the way *in*. Remember, the Knife of Cain keeps its power for the next century. I don't like to think of anybody getting his hands on it."

"You mean we don't tell anybody about

the underground city and the rest?" asked Herman.

"I hate to say it, but that's just what I mean," said Indy. "Ordinarily, it would be our duty to share our knowledge with the world. That's what any good archeologist would do. But there are times when learning has to take a back seat to mankind. This is one of them."

"It sure is," Herman agreed, thinking of the knife lying there underground. It made him shiver. He'd be glad to forget it.

Then he said, "Now that that's settled, how do we make it to Konya? You don't happen to have a magic carpet, do you?"

"I've got something better," said Indy. He pulled a cloth bag from under his robe. He shook it. It made a clinking sound. "Gold coins. Part of the count's tribute to the king. I picked them up before we took off. I figured they might come in handy."

Then Indy spotted a couple of men riding camels in the distance.

He yelled at them at the top of his lungs, *"Hey, taxi!"*

# Chapter 16

Two days later, two camels came to a halt in front of the best hotel in Konya. Each camel carried two people. But the loads were not too heavy. One of the riders on each camel was a young boy.

A flick of the camel drivers' whips, and both camels lowered themselves to their knees. The boys climbed off. Then the boys and the drivers shook hands warmly. One of the boys handed a driver a bag that clinked loudly as the driver stuffed it into his saddle pouch.

*"Tesekkurederim."* The drivers thanked the boys, with bows of their heads and big smiles.

*"Birsey degil,"* said Herman. He felt pleased as punch that he remembered how to say "You're welcome." There was a lot to be said for learning foreign words. It made you feel better, smarter. That was one of the things that this trip had taught him. One of the many things.

*"Allahhaismarladik!"* both drivers said.

"That means 'Allah go with you,' " Indy said to Herman. "You say that when you leave somebody."

As the drivers rode off, Indy called after them, *"Gule gule."* That was what you said to a person going away.

Suddenly, from behind them, a voice said, "So you boys have learned a bit of the language. Good to see you have not entirely wasted your time here."

It was Indy's dad.

Indy's brain started racing. He wasn't worried that his dad might have noticed they were missing. That was one thing he could

117

count on with his dad. When Professor Jones was buried in research, the whole world could vanish and he wouldn't notice.

But Indy hadn't counted on his dad's spotting Herman and him before they had a chance to change back into their regular clothes. How could they explain the robes they were wearing?

Indy needn't have worried.

"I see you boys have been playing Arab. In a sandbox, it would seem," his dad said. Indy groaned to himself. His dad still imagined Indy was somewhere between three and five years old.

"Yeah. Right. It was loads of fun," said Indy. He shot a warning glance at Herman to keep a straight face.

"I see I was right to make sure you had a friend on this trip," Professor Jones went on. "You were no trouble at all. I was able to get a pile of work done. What beautiful, beautiful manuscripts they have here. I discovered a vast amount."

"Good to hear that," Indy said.

"Someday you, too, will find out how much

you can discover in books," Indy's dad said. "All the buried secrets of the past. Of course, you have a lot of growing up to do before then."

"I can hardly wait," Indy sighed.

"As for me, I can hardly wait to get home," said Herman. "I mean, all these wide-open spaces have been fine. But I kind of miss my crowded old house."

"Well, it won't be long now," Professor Jones said. "We leave for America tomorrow."

"You've finished all your research?" said Indy, surprised. He had figured his dad would keep feasting on books for weeks.

"Not entirely," Professor Jones admitted. "But as I said, I did get a great deal done. And something has come up that has me worried."

"What's that?" asked Indy. It had to be something serious, very serious, to make his dad take notice.

"The librarian told me about it," Professor Jones said. "He reads all the latest papers. It seems the heir to the throne of Austria-

Hungary was shot to death. In some tiny town in the Balkans called Sarajevo. It's caused a lot of anger. Some hotheads are even talking about war. And Turkey could become involved."

"The war your dad said couldn't happen," Indy said to Herman.

Herman nodded. He knew now what strange things could happen in the world. That was another thing this trip had taught him.

"I agree with Herman's father," said Professor Jones. "I feel sure it will all soon blow over. Just a tempest in a teapot. If I were alone here, I wouldn't give it a thought. But I feel a responsibility for you boys. I don't want to expose you to even a hint of danger. Better safe than sorry."

"Dad, when did this killing take place?" Indy asked. "The date, I mean."

"Let's see," said Professor Jones. He paused, then remembered. "June 28. But I just heard about it today. The papers here come late. Why do you ask?"

Indy shrugged. "No special reason." Then

he said, "You know, I have a hunch trouble really is brewing. Big trouble."

Herman nodded. "I have that hunch, too."

Indy's dad chuckled. "You boys and your hunches. Comes of reading adventure novels instead of history."

Neither Indy nor Herman felt like chuckling. Or even smiling.

"Yeah," said Indy. "Us boys and our hunches."

# HISTORICAL NOTE

Archduke Francis Ferdinand of Austria-Hungary was killed in Sarajevo on June 28, 1914. World War I broke out in August, and lasted until 1918. It was the most terrible war the world had ever known. And it planted the seeds of an even greater conflict, World War II, which lasted from 1939 to 1945. Even that war did not bring true peace, making this the most destructive century in history.

After World War I, the modern Turkish state was founded by the revered leader,

Kemal Ataturk. Constantinople was renamed Istanbul, which it remains today.

The underground cities of Cappadocia were discovered by accident in 1963. Since then, over thirty have been found. All are connected by miles of tunnels to form a single vast city. They been explored seven levels down, and some are open to tourists for four levels. But no one knows how big they are, how deep they go, who built them, or why. There has been no discovery of an ancient blackened knife. Not yet.

# TO FIND OUT MORE, CHECK OUT...

*Turkey...in Pictures* prepared by Steve Feinstein. Published by Lerner Publications, 1988. A fun-to-look-at book about Turkey that explains its history, culture, geography, and more. Maps, photographs, paintings—many in color.

*Buried Cities and Ancient Treasures* by Dora Jane Hamblin. Published by Simon and Schuster, 1973. How archaeologists discovered buried Turkish cities (other than Cappadocia) and mountain kingdoms of earlier centuries. The author's visits to the sites result in a "you-are-there" feeling. Maps, photographs, paintings.

"Cappadocia: Turkey's Country of Cones." Published in *National Geographic,* January 1958. See what Indy and Herman saw when they got to Cappadocia! A photographic essay about more recent residents and the aboveground "fairy chimneys" of the region. Maps and photographs.

"Keeping House in a Cappadocian Cave," by Jonathan S. Blair. Published in *National Geographic,* July 1970. Learn how the author and his wife lived in a hollowed-out cave, as ancient cliff dwellers did. (This is the kind of home Indy hid in.) A fascinating personal account. Maps and color photographs.